When we were young, my sister and I were always playing ghost games. Ghosts are invisible, we told each other, and so they could be anywhere – on your shoulders, hiding in your hair, tying a knot in your laces. Because of the ghosts, I was no good at Hide and Seek. Before anyone could count to ten, I always ran out and yelled, 'Here I am!' I couldn't stand the idea of a ghost breathing down my neck in the dark wardrobe where I was hiding. Now we're introducing you to some of these sticky, oozy ghosts...and look out for the white tigers, too...Grrr!

ANNA FIENBERG

Anna and Barbara Fienberg write the Tashi stories together, making up all kinds of daredevil adventures and tricky characters for him to face. Lucky he's such a clever Tashi.

Kim Gamble is one of Australia's favourite illustrators for children. Together Kim and Anna have made such wonderful books as *The Magnificent Nose and Other Marvels*, *The Hottest Boy Who Ever Lived*, the *Tashi* series, the *Minton* picture books, *Joseph,* and a full colour picture book about their favourite adventurer, *There once was a boy called Tashi.*

First published in 1996
This edition first published in 2006

Allen & Unwin
83 Alexander St
Crows Nest NSW 2065
Australia
Phone: (61 2) 8425 0100
Fax: (61 2) 9906 2218
Email: info@allenandunwin.com
Web: www.allenandunwin.com

National Library of Australia
Cataloguing-in-Publication entry:

Fienberg, Anna.
   Tashi and the ghosts.

   New cover ed.
   For primary school children.
   ISBN 978 1 74114 967 8.

   ISBN 1 74114 967 3.

   1. Children's stories, Australian. 2. Tashi (Fictitious character) – Juvenile
fiction. I. Fienberg, Barbara. II. Gamble, Kim. III. Title. (Series: Tashi; 3).

A823.3

Cover and series design by Sandra Nobes
Typeset in Sabon by P.I.X.E.L. Pty Ltd, Melbourne
Printed in Australia by McPhersons Printing Group

10 9 8 7 6 5 4 3 2 1

Tashi

and the GHOSTS

written by
Anna Fienberg

and

Barbara Fienberg

·

illustrated by
Kim Gamble

ALLEN & UNWIN

'Guess what Tashi is having for dinner
tonight,' said Jack, as he spooned up the
last strawberry.

'Roast leg of lion caught fresh from the
jungle,' Jack's father said keenly.
'Wrong!' Jack laughed.

'Grilled tail of snake caught fresh from the
desert,' his mother said proudly.
'Double wrong! He's having Ghost Pie, from
a special recipe that he learned from—'

'Ghosts!' cried Mum and Dad together.
'Right!' said Jack. 'And would you like to
know how he came by this spooky recipe?'
'Yes indeed,' said Mum.

'Can't wait,' said Dad, getting comfortable
on the sofa. 'So tell us. After Tashi tricked
those giants and teased the bandits, how did
he meet these *ghosts*?'

'Well, it was like this,' said Jack. 'The very night that Tashi escaped from the bandits' camp and ran home to his village, Third Uncle saw a ghost light shining in the forest.'

'What does a ghost light look like? How would I know if I saw one?' asked Mum nervously.

'Like a street lamp, without the post?'
guessed Dad.

Jack shook his head. 'No, Tashi said it was
more like a small moon, sending out rays of
light into the trees, like white spider threads.'

9

'Ooh, can you get tangled up in them?' shivered Mum.

'In a way,' said Jack. 'Ghost monsters can be sticky, and they tend to hang around, Tashi says. Well, the next night there were more ghost lights. They came closer, and closer, and Tashi called his parents to see. Soon the news spread through the village and everyone was peeping behind their curtains at the phantom lights flitting through the forest.

'In the morning the people hurried to the square to talk about the ghosts. Some wanted to pack their belongings and move right away. Others wanted to burn down the forest so the ghosts would have no place to live. Finally they decided to ask Wise-As-An-Owl what he thought would be the best plan.'

'*My* plan would be to ignore them,' said
Dad. 'If the ghosts got no attention, they'd
probably go away.'

'I don't think that works with ghosts, Dad,'
said Jack. 'Anyway, Wise-As-An-Owl told
the men to organise a great beating of
saucepan lids outside their houses that night
as soon as it grew dark. They did, and sure
enough, the ghosts slipped away, back into
the forest.

'But the next night the ghosts came back. They drifted up like smoke, nearer and nearer, until they were pressing their faces against the windows. Their mouths were huge and gluey, and the air in the houses began to grow stale and thin as they sucked at the keyholes and under the doors. Everybody in the village burst out into the streets, coughing and choking. Men and women thundered around making a great crashing noise with saucepans and garbage lids and firecrackers. The ghosts melted away but Tashi was sure that they weren't gone for long.'

'They'd have gone forever if people had ignored them,' muttered Dad. 'Who comes back for no attention?'

'Well,' continued Jack, 'in the morning Tashi went to see his father's Younger Brother. He lives up on a hill overlooking the village and spends his nights studying the stars through a great telescope that he built years ago.

'Tashi told him about the ghost monsters who were frightening the villagers and he cried, "Of course, I know why they have come now. Look, Tashi," and he took out his charts of the stars and his Book of Calculations. "You see, look here. In three days' time there will be an eclipse of the moon."'

'I'll bet Tashi didn't know what *that* was,'
Dad laughed. He was already looking for
the dictionary.

'Yes,' said Jack patiently. 'It's what happens
when the moon is blacked out for a while
by the shadow of the earth. Well, Younger
Brother said to Tashi, "Last time there was
an eclipse, the river flooded and your
father's pigs were drowned. And the time
before that we had a plague of locusts that
ate the village fields bare. You'll see, with
this next eclipse there will be a haunting of
ghosts."

'At that, Tashi thought "*Aha!*", and he began to form one of his cunning plans. He waited two more days and sure enough the saucepan lids did no good at all. Each night after the people went to bed, the ghosts floated back to the village. On the third night, a brave dog rushed out of his house but as he drew breath to bark, he sucked in a tendril of grey ghost, and it was terrible to see. He choked and gasped and his fine black coat grew pale and wispy until he was just a shadow, melting into the stones.

'The villagers drew their curtains against the sight of it, but Tashi crept out into the forest. At first he could see only the small moons of light, tangling amongst the leaves. But as he tip-toed into the dark heart of the forest, he saw the ghosts themselves.

18

'And there were hundreds of them—
hopping ghosts, prowling ghosts, gliding
ghosts. They were like white dripping
shadows, fat and thin, tall and tiny,
whipping all around him.

'Suddenly Tashi felt a cold weight on his head. "Oh no, a jumping ghost," he thought, and he tried to pull it off. But it slid down over his eyes and nose like sticky egg white, and he could hardly see or breathe. "Oh no, a jumping *and* slithering ghost," he groaned, as it trickled down his back and clamped his arms.

'"Let me go!" Tashi screamed, and as he screamed he sucked in a bit of cold eggy ghost. He felt as if he were choking, and then more and more ghosts pressed their bodies against him. Like thickening fog they crowded around and Tashi didn't want to breathe for fear of sucking in those damp whirling phantoms.

'And then a huge glowing ghost as big as a
ship loomed over him. Its eyes were empty,
and it was the meanest-looking ghost Tashi
had ever seen.'

'Has Tashi seen many ghosts before this?'
asked Dad.

'Yes, he's seen a few in his time, he says.
Well, this mean-looking, leader ghost asked
Tashi why he had come into the forest at
night.

'"I've come to warn you," Tashi hissed at him, blowing out wisps of ghost as he spoke. "If you don't leave our village at once, you will all suffer."

'The huge ghost laughed. The sound rippled like wind through the forest. "And how exactly will we suffer?"

'"Well," Tashi told him, "my friend the Red-Whiskered Dragon-Ghost will come and punish you if you hurt me or frighten the people in my village."

'There was a low buzz as the ghosts swarmed together, discussing Tashi's news. The smaller ghosts were trembling, and their outlines were fading a little with fear. But the leader ghost was scornful. "Why should we believe *you*? No one could hurt *us*!"

'"Oh, I can easily prove it," Tashi said. "Just look at the moon up there. See how round and full it is? Now I will call my friend, the Red-Whiskered Dragon-Ghost, and he will open his huge jaws and eat the moon right up. When the moonlight disappears you will know how great he is and you will be afraid."

'Tashi called out into the night, "O mighty Red-Whiskered Dragon-Ghost, when I count to three, please open your jaws and take your first gigantic bite out of the moon!"

'Tashi counted *o-n-e* very, very slowly. He was worrying, deep inside himself—what if Younger Brother was wrong with his calculations? Could an eclipse be late?

'He counted *t-w-o* even more slowly. Was the moon shrinking a little?

'"Are you ready, ghost monsters?" Tashi cried, and then he shouted, "*THREE!*" just as the black shadow of the earth moved across the moon and sliced off a great piece.

'The ghosts watched as the moon grew smaller and smaller until there was not even a needlepoint of light in the dark sky. The moon had been swallowed up.

'The ghosts moaned with fear and their sighs blew through the trees like a gale of ice. "Please," they cried to Tashi, "tell your friend to give us back the moon. Tell him to spit it out again!"

'Tashi was silent for a moment, letting the ghosts feel the awful weight of a sky without light. Their own little moons of ghost-light were paler now, swamped by the darkness of the night.

'"All right," Tashi said finally, "I will ask him to grant you your wish—if you do two things. First, you must all leave this part of the earth, and never come back. Every now and again, the Red-Whiskered Dragon-Ghost will gobble up the moon for a short time, just to remind you never to frighten my village and its people again."

'"Very well," the leader ghost grudgingly agreed. "And the second thing?"
'"You must give me the recipe for Ghost Pie. I have heard that it is delicious, and for three days after eating it a person can walk through solid walls."

'The ghost leader let out a roar of rage. The little ghosts quivered and faded into the trees. They were shrinking with every moment, hanging like cloudy raindrops from the forest leaves.

'"Ghost Pie is one of our greatest secrets," the leader ghost spat. He waved for some of the older ghosts to come closer. They whispered together and then the leader ghost turned to Tashi. "We will do as you say, young Tashi, if you promise never to reveal the ingredients to any other *living* soul."'

'Aha!' cried Dad, slapping his knee. 'So when are we going to have a taste of pie?'
'Tashi says we can all come over to dinner next Saturday to try it, as long as we don't ask any questions about how it is made,' said Jack.
'It's a promise,' beamed Dad. He stood up and stretched. 'Oh well,' he said, 'I suppose that's the end of the story, and Tashi's had no more trouble with ghosts then.'

'That's right,' smiled Jack, 'but only one moon went by before he was in a sticky situation with a truly wicked Baron!'

THE MOUNTAIN OF WHITE TIGERS

The doorbell rang.

'I'll go,' Jack called, because he knew who it would be. Tashi was spending the day with him, and they were going for a ferry ride. Jack had said to come early, in time for breakfast.

But when Tashi walked in, Mum peered at
his face with a worried frown. 'You look a
bit pale this morning, Tashi,' she said.
'Yes, I know,' sighed Tashi. I've been up
burping Ghost Pie all night.'

'Pancakes coming!' cried Dad from the
kitchen.
Tashi turned a little paler.

When they were all sitting around the table in the garden, and Tashi had managed three pancakes after all, Jack decided that he'd waited long enough. 'How did you meet this Wicked Baron?'

'Well, it was like this,' said Tashi. 'One day I went to visit Li Tam, my favourite auntie. I always like going to her place because she has the most interesting house in the village. The rooms are all decorated with painted scrolls and she lets me touch the delicate bowls and vases and hand-carved swords.'

'Does Li Tam do a lot of sword-fighting?'
asked Dad.

Jack rolled his eyes, but Tashi just smiled.
'No, the swords belonged to her father.
Anyway,' he went on, 'this particular day I
didn't even get a chance to knock on the
door, when it was flung open and out
stormed Li Tam's landlord, the wicked
Baron.'

'Aha!' cried Mum and Dad.

'Yes, he was grinding his gold teeth, and he pushed me out of the way. I picked myself up and as I dusted my pants off, I wondered why the Baron looked so angry.'

'Was he a friend of Li Tam's?' asked Dad.
'Oh no!' said Tashi. 'He was no one's
friend. The only thing he loved was gold.
You see, this Baron had once been poor, but
he had tricked an old banker out of his
riches, and then he had stolen some money
here and hired a few pirates there, until he
had a huge fortune.'

'Where did he keep all his gold?' asked
Mum.

'Well, it was a great mystery,' said Tashi.
'The people in the village were certain that
he had hidden it away in a deep cave. But
no one could be quite sure because the cave
lay at the top of The Mountain of White
Tigers.'

'I've never seen a white tiger,' said Dad, 'but
I've heard they are the fiercest kind.'

'Yes,' said Tashi. 'Anyway, Li Tam was very upset after the Baron stormed out. She told me that he had called to tell her that she would have to leave her home at once because he had been offered a good price for it. And Li Tam had cried out, "Why must you have *my* house? You own the whole village!" But the Baron had ordered her to pack her bags by the end of the week.

'"Look at this then!" Li Tam had told him, and she'd pulled a piece of paper from the hidden drawer in her cupboard. On it was written a promise from the old banker that she could stay in the house for as long as she pleased.

'The Baron's face had grown red and that is why he'd stormed out, knocking me over as he went. But Li Tam was worried. "Tashi," she said to me, "I just know he won't stop at this. He'll try to find a way to push me out of my home."

'And sure enough, the next day when I went to visit her, I found the house was alive with mice. And they were everywhere. All the tables and chairs, shelves and cupboards seemed to be moving, crawling with wriggling bodies. From under beds, inside wardrobes, came loud squeals and scratchings. Well, Li Tam ran to me and said, "Look what the Baron has done! He sent his servants during the night to tip sacks of mice in through the windows."

'"Don't worry, Auntie," I said, "I will fix it." I ran home for a bag of rice cakes. I crumbled them up and laid a trail of crumbs from Li Tam's house right up to the Baron's kitchen door. The mice scrambled after me, gobbling up the crumbs as they went. And soon it was the *Baron* who had a houseful of mice.

'He was furious—roaring like a bull with a bellyache!—and when he saw the villagers laughing at him behind their hands, he charged right into the square on market day and shouted to them, "Tomorrow is the day you pay your rent money. From now on, all your rent will be three times as much as before. Be sure to have the money ready!" The people were shocked. "What will we do?" they wailed. "We have nothing more to give!"

'When I ran to tell Li Tam she said, "Oh, Tashi, if only we had the money to buy our own houses, then we would never have to worry about the wicked Baron again."'

'Aha!' cried Mum and Dad and Jack together.

'Aha!' agreed Tashi. 'That's when I felt one of my clever ideas coming on. So that night, when the last light went out, I crept through the streets to the Baron's house and tapped on the kitchen window. Third Aunt, who was the Baron's cook, opened the door.

'"Auntie, please let me in," I whispered. I ran over to the table where I'd often sat on baking mornings and pulled away the rug that lay under it. There was a little door over a flight of steps leading down into darkness.

'"You can't go down there, Tashi," said Third Aunt. "That passage leads all the way to the Mountain of White Tigers, and no one has ever returned from there."
'"The Baron must have," I said, "so I expect I will manage it, too." Still, as I peered into the blackness below, I did feel just a little afraid.'

'I don't wonder,' shivered Dad. 'Sometimes I feel a little afraid just going to put the garbage out at night.'

'Well,' said Tashi, 'I stopped looking into the dark and I whispered, "Hand me your lamp, please, Auntie. I'll be back before the Baron comes down to his breakfast in the morning."

'The passage twisted and turned, winding like a rabbit's burrow deep into the earth. I held my lamp high, but I could only see a short way in front of me, and the blackness ahead looked like the end of the world.

'I must admit that once or twice I did think of going back. I had no idea how long I'd been walking, or how much time I had left.

'But at last I felt the ground slope upwards,
and I could feel my heart start thumping
hard as I climbed up the steep path—and
suddenly, at the top, I stopped. The path
was blocked. I held up my lamp and saw a
door, with a gold latch. I pulled at it and
whoosh!—the door swung open.

'I stepped out onto the Mountain of
White Tigers.
'My face tingled in the snowy air and I
looked nervously into the night. The lamp
showed me a path, but on each side of it
were tall black trees, and behind those trees
who knew *what* was waiting!

'But I couldn't bear to go back empty-handed. And just then, I heard a growl, deep as thunder. I peered into the dark, but I could see nothing, only hear a grinding of teeth, like stones scraping. The growling became roaring, and my ears were ringing with the noise, and then, right in front of me, a white shape came out from behind a tree, and then another and another. The tigers were coming!

'They came so close to me that I could see their whiskers, silver in the moonlight, and their great red eyes, glowing like fires. They were even fiercer than I had been told, and their teeth were even sharper in their dark wet mouths, but I was ready for them. Second Aunt had warned me that the one thing white tigers fear is fire.

'I took a big breath and swung my bright burning lamp round and around my head. I charged down the path roaring, "Aargh! Aargh!" till my lungs were bursting.

'The tigers stopped and stared at me. They must have thought I was a whirling demon, with circles of light streaking about their heads. They bared their teeth, growling like drums rolling. But I saw them flinch, their white coats shivering over their muscles, and slowly, one by one, they turned away, gliding back through the trees. Oh, I was so happy watching those white shapes disappearing! I ran on and there, looming up above me, was the mouth of the cave.

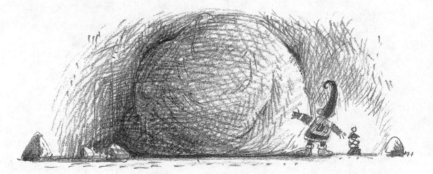

'The entrance was blocked by a huge stone boulder. I tried to squeeze through but the gap was too small.'

'Did you have to turn back then, Tashi?'
Jack held his breath.

'I thought for a moment I'd have to,' Tashi
nodded. 'But then I remembered that I'd
popped a piece of Ghost Pie into my pocket
before leaving home. I quickly nibbled a bit
and pushed at the boulder again. This time
my hand slid right through it and the rest of
me followed as easily as stepping through
shadows.

'I ran inside *whooping*! There were sacks and sacks of shiny, golden coins! Puffing and panting, I loaded them into a huge knapsack I had with me, and hauled it onto my back to carry.'

'I wish *I'd* been there to help you!' Jack said
wistfully.

'Me too,' said Tashi. 'That knapsack made
my knees buckle. And then, coming out of
the cave, I had to whirl my lamp round my
head and roar as well, just in case there
were still tigers lurking in the trees.'
'So how did you crawl back through the
tunnel with all that gold on your back?'
asked Mum.

'Well, it was like this,' said Tashi. 'I took the sack off my back and put it on the ground. Then I rolled it along with my feet. It was easier that way, but very slow. And of course I was getting very worried about the time.

'I crept back up the stairs and into the kitchen as it was growing light. Third Aunt was just putting a match to the kitchen fire, and she almost dropped the poker when she saw me.

'"What a clever Tashi," she cried, when she spied the gold.

'Well, I thanked her, but I wasn't finished
yet, oh no! I crept to each house in the
village and whispered a few words, passing
a little sack of gold through the windows.

'Next morning all the people were in the
square when the Wicked Baron arrived for
his rent. Wise-As-An-Owl stepped forward.
"Baron," he began, "our children who went
away to other parts for work have done
well and sent gold home to their families.
Now we would like to buy our houses."

'And all the villagers stepped up and poured the gold onto the table before the Baron. What a sight it was! The mountain of coins glittered so brightly in the morning sun that I had to turn my eyes away! But The Baron stared. He couldn't *stop* looking! Still, he was hesitating. He liked getting money every month from his rents, but he couldn't resist the sight of all those shining, winking coins. "Very well," he agreed, and I could tell he was itching to gather up the coins and run his fingers through them. "I'll sign right now," and he took the papers that Wise-As-An-Owl had ready for him.

'That night there was a great feast with music and dancing to celebrate the new freedom of the village. My grandmother and Second Aunt were singing so loudly, that only I heard the faint bellow of rage coming from the Mountain of White Tigers.'

'Oh well,' said Dad, 'that wicked Baron got what he deserved, eh, Tashi? And I suppose all the village people were happy and contented from that day on.'

'Oh yes,' agreed Tashi, 'and so was I, until I came face to face with the Genie. But now we'd better go—if we don't run all the way we'll miss the ferry! Are you coming, Jack?' And the two boys raced out the door, as if the Genie itself were after them.